Sarah's Willow

By Friedrich Recknagel

Illustrated by Maja Dusíková

Translated by Anthea Bell

North-South Books

New York / London

An old willow tree grew by the pond behind Sarah's house. Sarah and her friend Mary often went there. They liked to play under the willow better than anywhere else.

But one day Sarah saw two men beside the pond. One of them painted a big cross on the tree trunk. Was he allowed to do that?

When Sarah was in bed that evening, she kept thinking about those two men.

She had heard one of them saying: "Yes, this one, too." And what did the cross mean?

At last Sarah fell asleep.

Sarah dreamed of her willow tree. Suddenly, a ghostly little figure appeared, hovering in the air before her. Sarah shivered in fright. Then, plucking up her courage, she asked: "Who are you?"

"Who are you?" Sarah repeated.

"I'm a tree spirit," said the ghostly figure.
"I live in this willow."

Sarah was too surprised to answer.

"I know you," the tree spirit went on. "Your name is Sarah. I was always glad to see you here."

"Well, I'm here again now," said Sarah, "but you look sad."

"I'm very sad," said the tree spirit.
"Have you seen this cross on the trunk?"

Sarah stared at the mark on the tree trunk.
It shone with a strange glow. It grew bigger and
bigger. . . . And then, suddenly, Sarah's dream
was over.

The next day Sarah hurried home from school. She was quite breathless by the time she reached the pond. And then she had a terrible shock.

She stopped and stared in horror. There on the ground lay her willow. It had been cut down. Four men were loading their tools into their truck.

"Time to knock off work for today," said one of the men. "We'll finish the job tomorrow." Then they all climbed into their truck and drove off.

Sarah couldn't believe it.
She sat down on the tree trunk and cried and cried.
At last she trudged sadly home.

Sarah found her father in the kitchen.

"You look terrible!" he said. "Have you been crying?"

Sarah told him what had happened.

"That's too bad," said Father. He rubbed his chin and murmured, "Hm, hm."

Suddenly he said, "Come along, let's go out and look at the willow. Bring your watering can and your little spade."

Sarah didn't know what her father
was planning to do, but she went to
find her watering can and her spade.
Then they both walked down to the
pond.

"Ah," said Father, when they reached the willow. "Now I can see why they had to cut the tree down. It was sick, and it wouldn't have lived much longer anyway. But we can do something about that! I have a good idea."

He cut a slender twig from the old willow. Then he told Sarah to dig a hole. Father planted the twig in the hole and Sarah filled it with earth. After that they both trod the ground down firmly with their feet.

"There, now you must water it well," said Father. Sarah scooped some water out of the pond and poured it over the twig. On the way home she didn't feel sad anymore.

After that, Sarah visited the little twig they
had planted every day. She watered it carefully.
Often her friend Mary came with her.

One day the two girls saw new little leaves sprouting from the tips of the twig.

"The tree spirit has moved in!" cried Sarah happily.

"Will we be able to play underneath the tree soon?" asked Mary.

"Oh, no," Sarah told her. "It will take a long time to grow. But now we have to make sure the tree spirit feels happy in its new home. That's what my father said."

"Is there really a tree spirit living there?" Mary wondered.

"Of course," said Sarah cheerfully. "I know there is. I saw the tree spirit in a dream, and now it's back again!"

Copyright © 2001 by Nord-Süd Verlag AG, Gossau Zürich, Switzerland.
First published in Switzerland under the title *Sarahs Weide*.
English translation copyright © 2002 by North-South Books Inc.

First published in the United States, Great Britain, Canada,
Australia, and New Zealand in 2002 by North-South Books,
an imprint of Nord-Süd Verlag AG, Gossau Zürich, Switzerland.
Distributed in the United States by North-South Books Inc., New York.

Library of Congress Cataloging-in-Publication Data is available.
A CIP catalogue record for this book is available from The British Library.
ISBN 0-7358-1527-5 (trade binding)
1 3 5 7 9 TB 10 8 6 4 2
ISBN 0-7358-1528-3 (library binding)
1 3 5 7 9 LB 10 8 6 4 2
Printed in Germany

For more information about our books, and the authors and artists
who create them, visit our web site: www.northsouth.com